For Paul, with love
—S.H.

To Kevin Lewis, for always rooting for me
—M.C.

Printed in Malaysia

First Edition

1 3 5 7 9 10 8 6 4 2

H106-9333-5-13319

Library of Congress Cataloging-in-Publication Data

Hood, Susan, 1954–

Rooting for you : (a moving up story) / Susan Hood ; illustrated by Matthew Cordell.—1st ed.

p. cm.

Summary: A seed, afraid but bored in the dark soil, decides to put out one little root, then one little shoot,
before learning that there are plenty of friends around for encouragement.

ISBN 978-1-4231-5230-9

[1. Seeds—Fiction. 2. Growth—Fiction.] I. Cordell, Matthew, 1975– ill. II. Title.

PZ7.H763315Roo 2013

[E]—dc23   2012006712

Designed by Sara Gillingham Studio.

Text is set in Archer and Futuramano.

Reinforced binding

Visit www.disneyhyperionbooks.com

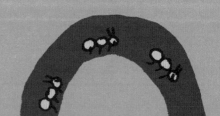

Rooting for you

Susan Hood ❀ Illustrated by Matthew Cordell

Disney • HYPERION BOOKS • NEW YORK

I am NOT

coming out!

It's DARK out there.

You never know
who might be digging...

...in the DARK.

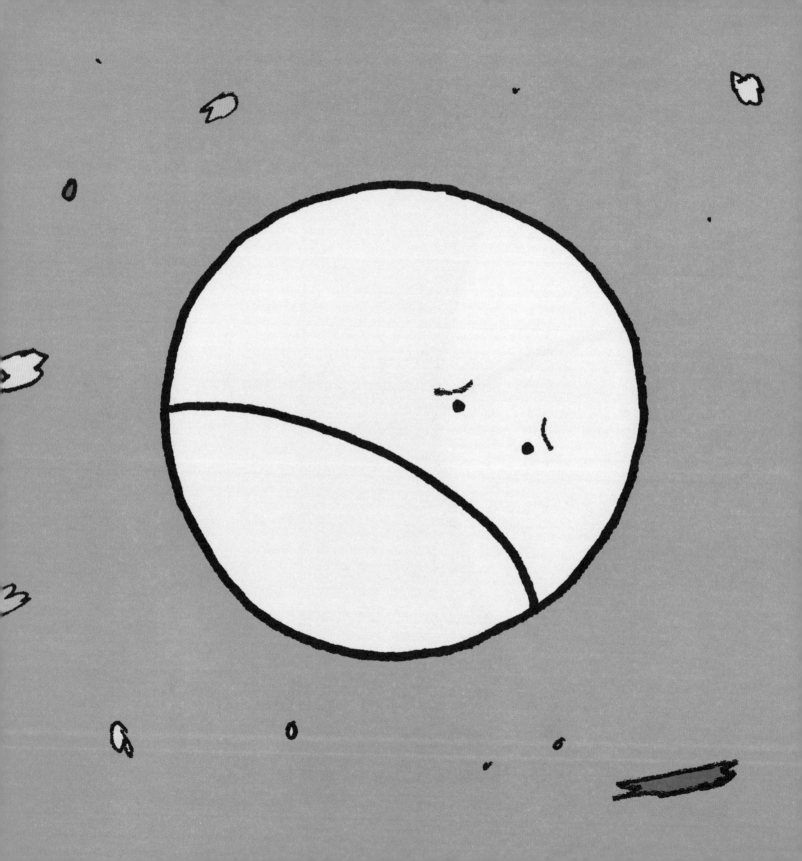

There might be **monsters**

beneath my bed....

Hard, cold eyes

and snickering snouts...

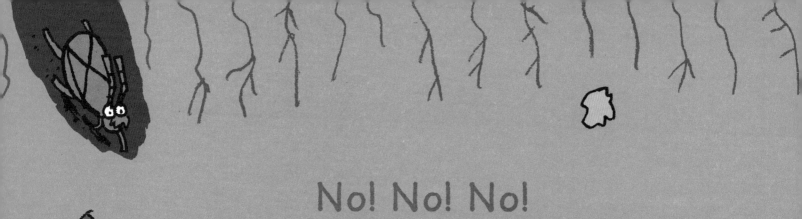

No! No! No!
I am NOT coming out!

Safe and sound,
down,
down,
down,
here in the ground
on my own,

all alone.

I'm BORED!

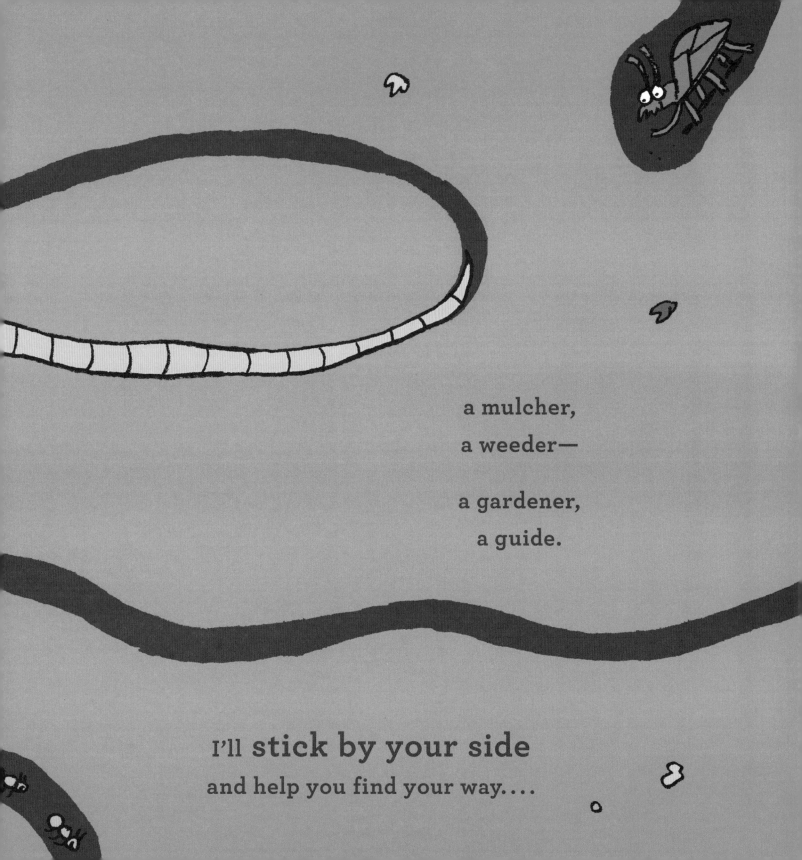

a mulcher,
a weeder—

a gardener,
a guide.

I'll **stick by your side**
and help you find your way....

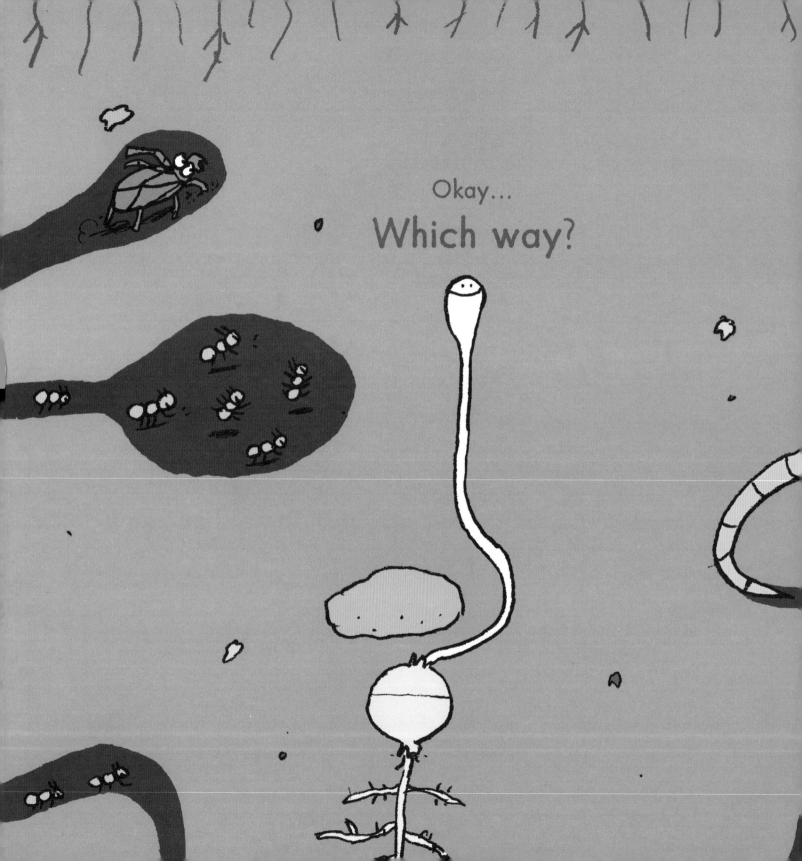

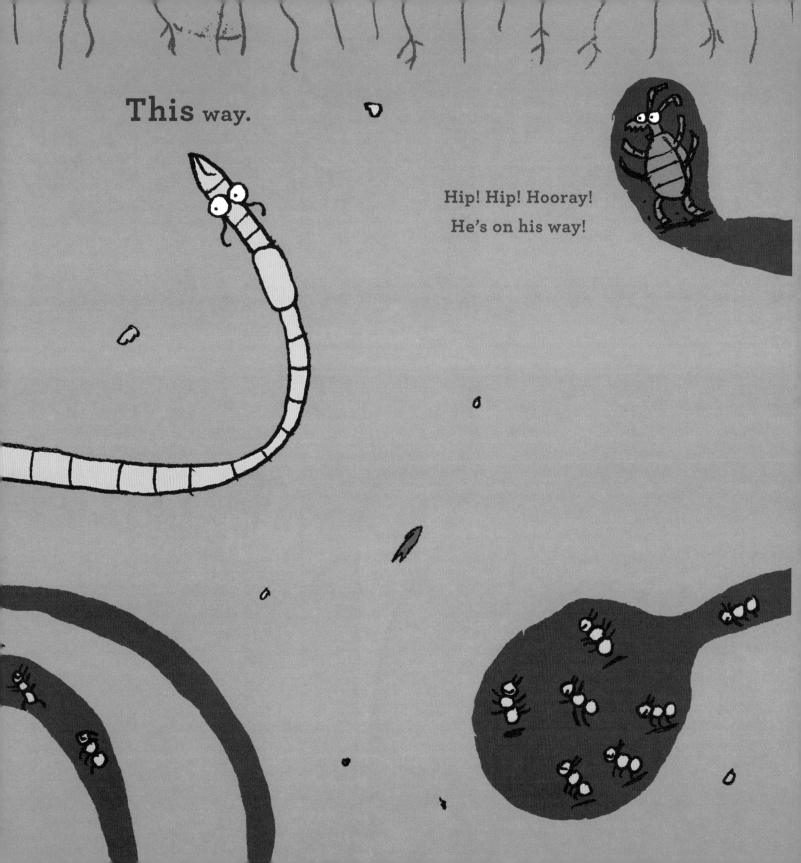

Uh-oh!

Oh, no!

Where do I go?

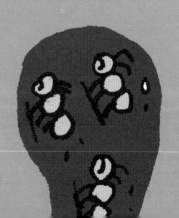

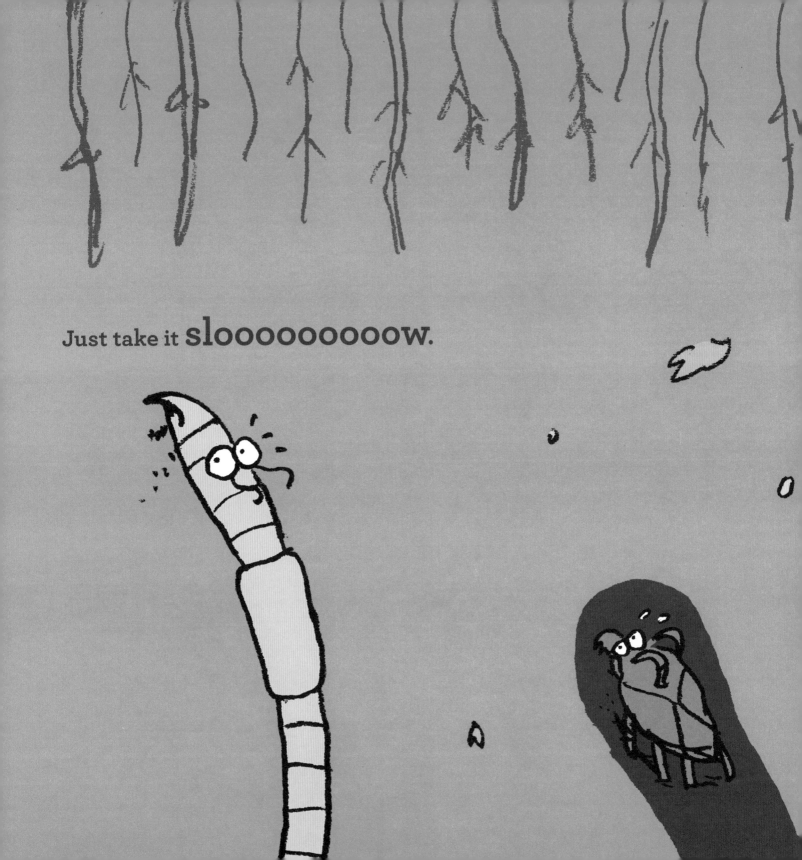

I'm getting scared!
It's light up there.
You never know who might be lurking
in the LIGHT!

There might be **monsters**
above my head.
Hard cold eyes...

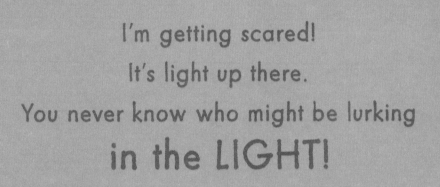

**OR
soft warm skies!**

With room to bloom,
to stand up straight.
Get going, get growing!
Your whole life awaits!

There are friends to feed you,
friends to weed you,
and friends indeed who
really need you!

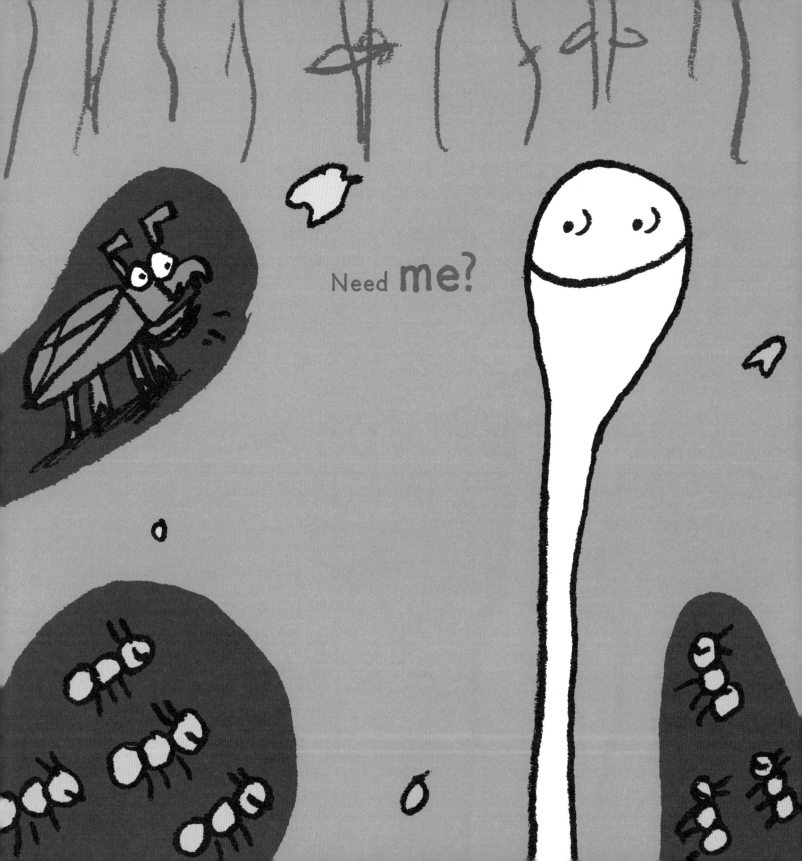

Yes, YOU!

You've lots to do.

You've talent to share.

Go soak up the sun.

Let your breath fill the air.

It's time you got to it!

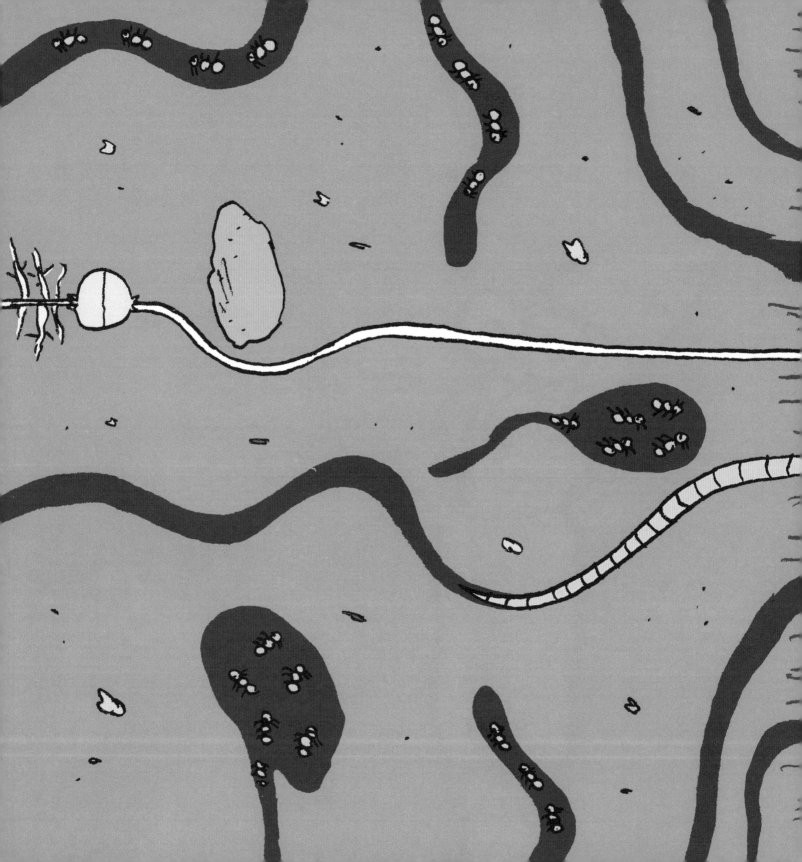

Okay!

I CAN DO IT!

Here I...

G...R...O...O...O...O...O...W!

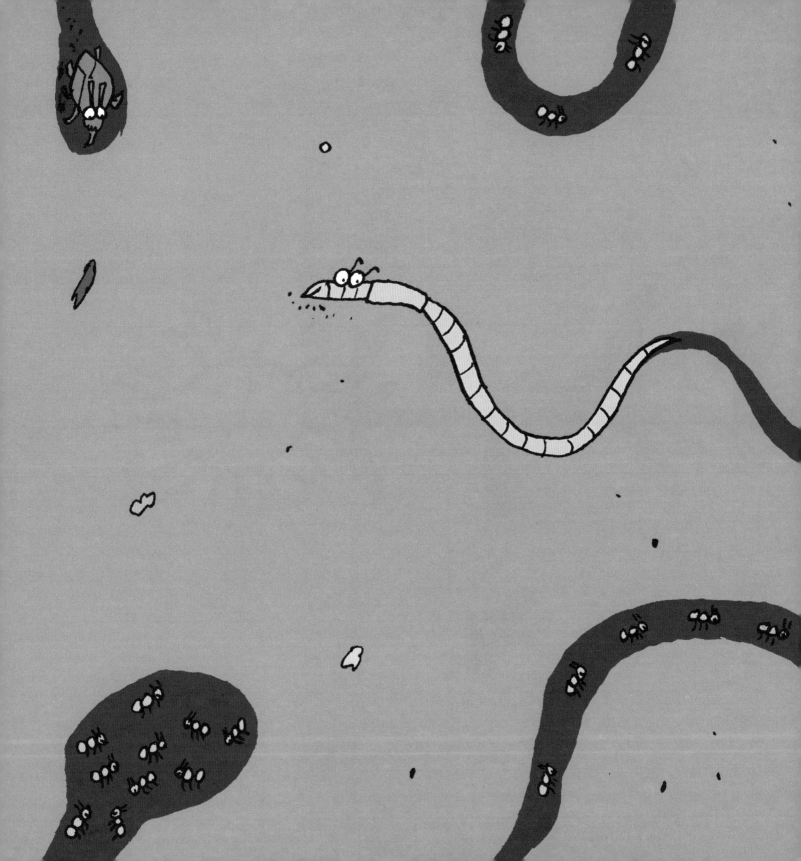